OLYMPIA

ON THE BALL

SHOO RAYNER

ORCHARD

CHAPTER ONE

"Good luck, Nik!" Olly yelled to his favourite athlete, who was getting ready to play the exciting Greek ball game called *episkyros*.

Olly's dad ran the gymnasium in Olympia, the town where the Olympic Games were held every four years. Olly worked at the gym, helping athletes and learning sporting skills from them.

The athletes had been training hard for the Olympics all week and now they were playing *episkyros* for a bit of fun.

The two teams faced each other on the halfway line and Olly's dad, Ariston, threw the ball high into the air to start the match.

The rules of *episkyros* were simple. Players had to pass the ball to each other and try to touch it down in the other team's half to gain a point. If a player dropped the ball in his own half, the other team won a point.

Nik caught the ball and stood just short of the halfway line, ready to pass it. Damon, who was an athlete on the other team, towered in front of him. The two men stared into each other's eyes, daring the other one to make the first move.

"Get him, Damon!" Spiro called.

Spiro worked at the gym with Olly. They rarely agreed on anything and were not exactly the best of friends.

"Pass the ball, Nik!" Olly shouted.

If Nik passed the ball, he'd be safe. Players were allowed to tackle the person holding the ball, and although murder wasn't allowed, *episkyros* could be quite dangerous! Olly didn't want to see his hero turned into mincemeat.

Damon was light on his feet for such a giant of a man. In a flash he grabbed Nik and tried to trip him up so that the ball touched the ground.

Nik's face turned a shade of purple as he struggled to get free.

"Damon! Damon! Damon!" Spiro chanted.

"Pass the ball!" Olly shouted again. It was terrible to watch his hero losing like this.

But Nik couldn't pass the ball. Damon had his arms gripped in a vice-like lock.

Suddenly, Nik lost his balance and the two athletes crashed to the ground. There was a loud pop as they fell. Damon and Nik untangled themselves. A limp leather rag lay in the dust. They had crushed the life out of the ball!

Damon and Nik collapsed in howls of laughter, slapping each other on the back. They were good friends really!

Ariston picked up the ball and examined it. "Game over!" he announced. "Olly, throw this in the rubbish, will you? It's not worth mending any more. We'll use a new one next time."

Olly looked at the flat ball. It didn't look that broken to him. "Can I have it?" he asked. "I'm sure I could fix it so us kids can play with it later."

Ariston smiled at his son's enthusiasm. "Well, if you think you can mend it," he said, "you're welcome to have it."

"If you can fix it," Spiro taunted, "I'll show you how *episkyros* is really played!"

Olly smiled. He knew exactly what to do. Soon he would be the proud owner of a nicely mended ball.

CHAPTER TWO

"Hey, Linos! Wake up!" Olly yelled
as he charged around the back of
the Temple of Hermes. People from
Olympia sacrificed animals at the
temple, hoping the gods would give
them good luck. Olly knew the temple
butcher would be there, snoozing in
the shade.

Linos brushed a fly off the end of his nose and scowled at Olly. "Leave me alone," he moaned. "I've had a very busy morning."

The evidence was all around him. Piles of animal guts hummed in the corner as a million flies buzzed over them.

"I need a big bladder to blow up inside my *episkyros* ball," Olly said.

"No one has sacrificed anything larger than a goat for the past month," Linos complained. "It's all chickens, chickens, chickens these days. How anyone expects to have good luck by sacrificing something as lowly as a chicken, I don't know!"

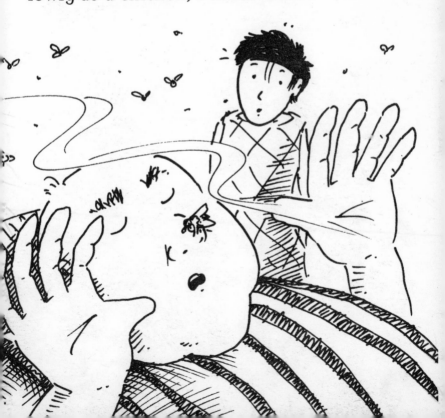

Olly was disappointed. "How am I going to get my *episkyros* ball blown up again, then?" he sighed.

"When I was young, we filled them with feathers," Linos said. "Feathers are as light as air and I've got bags of them over there. I've been plucking chicken feathers all morning!"

A smile crept over Olly's face. "It's better than nothing," he laughed. "Can I use one of your knives to cut the stitching in the leather?"

"Sure, but don't cut yourself!" said Linos, who hadn't lifted a finger since Olly had arrived.

Olly carefully cut the stitching and unthreaded it so he could get his hand inside the leather ball.

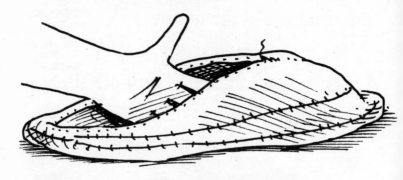

He pulled out the old, dried-up ox bladder that had burst...

...then stuffed the ball full of feathers until he couldn't fit any more in.

"Thanks, Linos!" Olly said when he had finished.

Linos waved a hand. "Don't mention it!"

Olly found his sister, Chloe, sitting in the shade under an acacia tree, where she was mending some old clothes.

"Could you sew this up for me, Chloe?" Olly asked. "Then I can have a game with the boys this evening, when it's a bit cooler."

Chloe looked at her precious
needle. It was carved out of fragile
bone. She only ever used it on soft
fabrics. The *episkyros* ball was made
of tough leather.

"I can't," she said. "My needle will
break if I sew that together."

"Oh, please!" Olly begged his sister.
"Look, the holes are already there. You
don't need to make any new ones."

Chloe wasn't sure. "I'll try, but if the needle breaks you'll have to find me another one from somewhere. They don't grow on trees, you know!"

She threaded the needle with fresh twine. "And I'll do it on one condition..." she said. "That you'll let me play on your team."

"What! But...!"

Chloe was just as sporty as her brother, and better than him at some things. But girls weren't allowed to compete at sport in Olympia, so Chloe was often left out of the boys' games.

"Oh, all right," Olly grumbled. "But the other boys might not like it!"

"I can look after myself," Chloe said, smiling to herself as she put the finishing touches to the *episkyros* ball.

She threw it to Olly. "Catch!"

CHAPTER THREE

"I've been looking for you!" Spiro called to Olly a little later that morning. "We're late. We should be laying the tables for the athletes' lunch." It was one of the boys' daily jobs at the gym.

"I was fixing my ball," Olly said, showing it to Spiro. "I didn't realise the time!"

"Let's have a look!" Spiro grabbed the ball from Olly. "It's heavier than usual," he growled. Then a sly grin crept over his face. "Meet me at the courtyard at sundown. My team will thrash the pants off you!"

Spiro threw the ball hard back to Olly and turned in the direction of the dining room.

Olly clutched the ball tightly. He was determined to beat Spiro!

Olly was carrying a watermelon
through from the kitchen when the
athletes came into the dining room
for lunch. Nik grabbed hold of it and
threw it to Damon.

Damon laughed and passed it back, over Olly's head. The athletes often teased the boys. The watermelon was passed all around the room before it was thrown back to Olly. It was heavy, but Olly caught it and held it above his head in triumph. The athletes roared their approval!

A gentle cough brought the room back to order. Simonedes, the athletes' history teacher, was standing behind his podium. Every day, while the athletes ate, he told stories of the Greek gods and heroes and all the things they got up to. Simonedes was a wonderful storyteller. Olly could listen to him all day.

"Orpheus was the most talented musician who ever lived," Simonedes began. "No one could resist the beauty of his music. Even the animals followed him when he played.

"When Orpheus fell in love with the beautiful Euridice, she agreed to marry him the moment she heard him play. But a short while later, Euridice was bitten by a viper and died a horrible death."

A murmur ran around the room, and Olly imagined how painful that would be.

"Orpheus was very upset," Simonedes continued. "He decided to follow his true love to Hades – the land of the dead. However, the gates of Hades were guarded by Kerberos, the three-headed dog, so that no living person could enter. But when Orpheus played his music, Kerberos was charmed and fell asleep."

Olly wished he could make Spiro's dog, who was also called Kerberos, lie down and go to sleep as easily. Kerberos had it in for Olly and was always trying to bite chunks out of him!

Simonedes continued, "When Orpheus met Pluto, the ruler of Hades, he softened his cold heart with music, and brought tears to his cruel eyes.

"Orpheus wasn't greedy. He didn't ask for Euridice to be given back to him. Instead he asked if Pluto would lend her to him for a year and a day. Pluto agreed – but only on one condition…"

Simonedes paused, and the athletes held their breath. "Euridice would follow Orpheus out of Hades, but if Orpheus looked back, even once, to check that Euridice was following, then he would lose her for ever."

Olly had heard this story many times before, but he couldn't wait for Simonedes to reveal the tragic ending.

Simonedes took a deep breath and sighed. "All the way along the twisting, winding path, and all the way up, up, up to the world of the living, Orpheus could hear Euridice's footsteps behind him. He was desperate to see his beloved again, but he never once looked behind him.

"As he came to the end of the tunnel and saw the sunshine and the living world so near at hand, Orpheus could wait no longer. He looked back – just to make sure that Euridice was still following. But he looked back too soon!

"Orpheus caught a glimpse of Euridice – a shadowy, waif-like image of the beautiful woman he loved so much. She slipped back and faded into the darkness. One word, weak and faint, drifted to his ears from her death-cold lips: 'Farewell!'"

The athletes were big and strong, but their hearts were soft. Tears rolled down Damon's cheeks as Simonedes finished his story.

"Orpheus was never allowed back into the land of the dead. He spent the rest of his life playing sad music, until he died and was finally able to join his one true love again."

Simonedes began rolling up his scroll book. Then he paused and raised an eyebrow.

"Remember, athletes!" he said loudly. "Never look back! Ahead of you lies victory – behind you, only defeat."

"Never look back," Olly repeated in a whisper so he wouldn't forget. "Ahead of you lies victory – behind you, only defeat."

40

CHAPTER FOUR

It was a blistering hot afternoon – too hot for Olly to do anything but lie in the shade and plan how he was going to beat Spiro at *episkyros*. He worked out some tactics in his mind.

When the orange sun sank below the hills and the hot afternoon became comfortably warm, Olly and Chloe went to the courtyard at the gym. A group of kids usually hung around there in the evenings, larking about and playing games. Spiro was already there.

"Look what I've got!" Olly called across the dusty yard. He spun the ball on the tip of his finger. "Anyone want to play *episkyros*?"

Spiro's dog, Kerberos, growled at the sight of Olly and fixed his hungry eyes on the ball.

Spiro stepped forward. "Olly and I will be captains!" he announced. "Now, let's choose teams. First, I choose Kerberos!"

"We're not playing against a dog!" Olly said.

Kerberos bared his teeth at Olly.

"Well, we're not playing against her!" Spiro sneered in Chloe's direction.

"Worried you might lose, Spiro?" Chloe jeered.

Spiro just grimaced at her.

After they had finished choosing their teams, Spiro shouted, "First team to ten points is the winner!" He grabbed the ball out of Olly's hands, ran across the line and scored. "This will be easy!" he laughed. "One, nil!"

"But we haven't started yet!" Olly said angrily.

Spiro squared up to Olly and glared at him. "Oh yes we have!"

Kerberos growled in agreement.

The teams were quite even. The skill of Olly's team was matched by the brawn of Spiro's team. Kerberos joined in the fun, yapping, barking and chasing the ball as it was passed from player to player.

Chloe was nimble on her feet. She found clear spaces in Spiro's half, allowing Olly to throw the ball forward to her so she could touch the ground and score points.

Soon Olly's team had nine points to Spiro's seven. Only one point more to win the game! Spiro's team sensed the possibility of defeat and began to play rough.

Olly caught the ball and took in the situation. Chloe was nearly in position.

"Hold on a second," Olly muttered to himself.

Just then, Kerberos barked.

"Look out behind you, Olly!" Spiro yelled.

Like Orpheus, Olly looked back. He thought Kerberos was about to sink his vicious teeth into his leg! Spiro leaped forward, snatched the ball from his hands and scored a point.

"Hey! That's cheating!" Olly cried.

"All's fair in sport and war!" Spiro laughed. "That's nine points to eight – we're still going to beat you, Olly!"

CHAPTER FIVE

The game started again and Olly caught the ball. He looked around the yard and saw Chloe running towards a clear position on the other side of the line. He just needed one more point!

"Hold on for just a second!" Olly urged himself.

Kerberos barked again.

"Olly!" Spiro bellowed. "Look out! He's right behind you!"

Olly felt his blood turn to ice. He knew exactly what Kerberos would like to do to him! He looked back, just in case, and lost concentration.

Once again, Spiro grabbed the ball from his hands and scored the equalising point. Spiro fell to the floor in hysterics. "Ha, ha, ha! Nine all! You never learn, Olly – your team is going down!"

Chloe stood over Spiro with her hands on her hips. She had a look on her face that could turn a boy to stone.

Spiro scrambled to his feet again. Chloe was the only person who wasn't scared of him. It made Spiro feel uneasy.

Olly could taste victory and was determined not to lose this chance. He caught the ball and paused to see who he should pass to. Spiro was lumbering towards him, ready to tackle.

"Keep your nerve!" Olly hissed to himself.

Then, again, Kerberos barked.

"Look out, Olly!" Spiro yelled. "He's right behind you!"

At last, Olly remembered Simonedes' words. *Never look back. Ahead of you lies victory – behind you, only defeat.*

"I'm not falling for that trick again," Olly sneered.

Spiro lunged at him and grabbed the ball. The two boys began an epic tussle. Neither of them wanted to lose!

Kerberos saw that his master needed help. He raced towards the two boys, drooling spit from his mouth.

"Spiro! Behind you!" Chloe screamed. The look of horror on her face made Spiro look back.

Olly saw a mouth full of vicious teeth flying through the air towards them. Instinctively, he threw himself to one side.

Spiro stood wide-eyed and gormless, holding the ball in front of him.

Kerberos's powerful jaws grabbed the ball from Spiro's hands and he sailed through the air in a graceful arc, right over the line and into Spiro's half.

Kerberos landed with a thump and skidded through the dust. He shook his head from side to side as if he was trying to kill the ball.

The crazy dog shredded the leather cover to bits. Feathers filled the air.

CHAPTER SIX

Soon there were feathers *everywhere*.
It looked as if winter had arrived and
covered everything in snow!

Kerberos looked like a giant chicken.
He spat and coughed, trying to clear
the fluffy down from his throat.

"Game abandoned!" Spiro announced in a matter-of-fact tone of voice.

"Excuse me!" said Chloe . "I think you'll find we won!"

"Ha! Ha! Come on," Spiro waved to his team-mates, "let's go and find something else to do."

"Kerberos was on your team," Chloe insisted. "He carried the ball over to your side of the line before it touched the ground."

"That makes it ten – nine to us!"
Olly said triumphantly. "We won!"

"Well, let's call it a draw, then!"
Spiro argued.

"NO!" said Chloe firmly. "It was the
winning point. We won!"

Spiro never knew what to say to Chloe. He could threaten any of the other boys with just a look, but Chloe was immune to his bullying. He dropped his shoulders in defeat.

"Nice one, sis!" Olly slapped Chloe's hand in a high five.

"It's so unfair!" Spiro grumbled as he walked away into the gloomy twilight. Kerberos trotted alongside him, his tail high in the air. He was proud of himself for defending his master from such a dangerous, feathery animal!

"All's fair in sport and war!" Olly yelled after Spiro, as the outline of his arch-enemy slowly faded into the darkness.

61

Olly smiled to himself. He had
heard the tale of Orpheus in the land
of the dead a thousand times before,
but when Simonedes told stories, Olly
always learned something new.

Olly whispered
Simonedes' words to
himself again, so
he wouldn't forget
the old man's
wisdom. "Never
look back. Ahead
of you lies victory
– behind you,
only defeat."

From now on,
Olly would keep
his sights fixed
firmly on victory!

OLYMPIC FACTS!

DID YOU KNOW...?

The ancient Olympic Games began over 2,700 years ago in Olympia, in southwest Greece.

The ancient Games were held in honour of Zeus, king of the gods, and were staged every four years at Olympia.

Episkyros was not an Olympic sport. It was played for fun to create a good team spirit among athletes.

The *episkyros* ball could be filled with anything light, like feathers, straw, or sponges from the sea.

The ancient Olympics inspired the modern Olympic Games, which began in 1896 in Athens, Greece. Today, the modern Olympic Games are still held every four years in a different city around the world.

OLYMPIA

SHOO RAYNER

RUN LIKE THE WIND	978 1 40831 187 5
WRESTLE TO VICTORY	978 1 40831 188 2
JUMP FOR GLORY	978 1 40831 189 9
THROW FOR GOLD	978 1 40831 190 5
SWIM FOR YOUR LIFE	978 1 40831 191 2
RACE FOR THE STARS	978 1 40831 192 9
ON THE BALL	978 1 40831 193 6
DEADLY TARGET	978 1 40831 194 3

All priced at £4.99